This
Treasure Cove Story
belongs to

BACKYARD BALLET

A CENTUM BOOK 978-1-912396-85-6
Published in Great Britain by Centum Books Ltd.
This edition published 2018.

1 3 5 7 9 10 8 6 4 2

Centum Books Ltd, 20 Devon Square, Newton Abbot,
Devon, TQ12 2HR, UK.

www.centumbooksltd.co.uk | books@centumbooksltd.co.uk
CENTUM BOOKS Limited Reg.No. 07641486.

Editorial and design assistance: Laurel Norman.

A CIP catalogue record for this book is available
from the British Library.

Printed in China.

nickelodeon

A Treasure Cove Story

Adapted by Mary Tillworth
Based on the teleplay 'Backyard Ballet' by Lacey Dyer
Illustrated by Liana Hee

Leah and Zac were twirling and leaping around Leah's living room. They had just seen *Swan Lake* and they were practising to put on their own ballet!

Leah spun and lost her balance. Zac crashed into the sofa!

'I guess we need to practise more,' Leah giggled.

Zac grinned. 'How about you practise spinning and I practise leaping? Later we can dance Swan Lake together!'

After Zac left to practise on his own, Leah sighed.
'If only I could dance like the real Swan Queen.'
Suddenly, she had an idea!

Leah summoned Shimmer and Shine, twin genies-in-training who could grant her three wishes a day.

'I wish I was the Swan Queen!' Leah declared.

'*Boom, Zahramay!* First wish of the day!' chanted Shine.

Leah found herself dressed as the Swan Queen from the ballet – but with six loud swans as royal subjects!

'I was hoping to spin like the *ballerina* Swan Queen, not be the actual queen of six swans!' she said.

Shine frowned. 'Oh, it sounds like I made a mistake.'

Leah smiled. 'It's okay, Shine. Sometimes mistakes happen. Maybe these swans won't get in the way of spinning practice!'

But having six swans in Leah's living room
turned into a giant honking disaster!

Leah had to get the swans outside before
they destroyed the whole house.

'I wish the swans would follow me!' she cried.

Shimmer jangled her
magic bracelets. '*Boom,
Zahramay!* Second
wish of the day!'

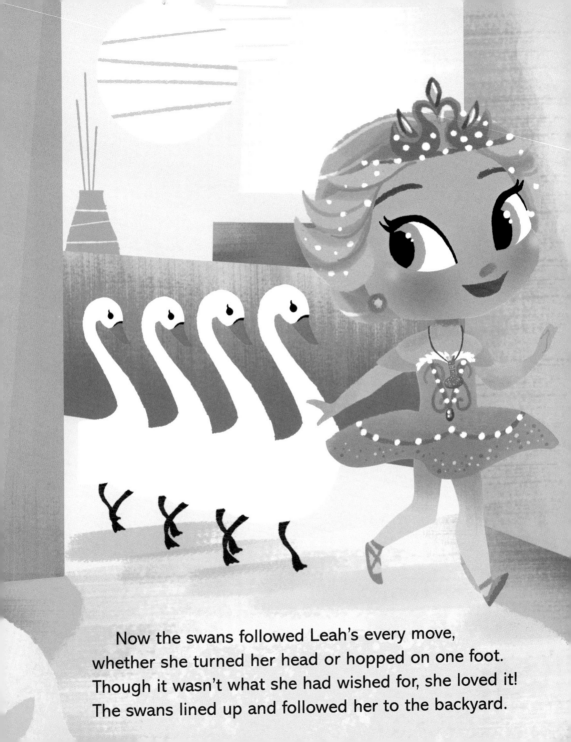

Now the swans followed Leah's every move,
whether she turned her head or hopped on one foot.
Though it wasn't what she had wished for, she loved it!
The swans lined up and followed her to the backyard.

Leah had saved her home from the swans, but she had forgotten to practise for the ballet performance!

She closed her eyes and made her final wish.
'I wish to be a ballerina in *Swan Lake*!'

When Leah opened her eyes, she was standing on a rock, surrounded by lily pads. Her backyard had been transformed into a giant lake!

She looked around. 'This is beautiful, but I wanted to dance like the ballerina from *Swan Lake*, not have an actual lake.'

Shine hung her head. 'Sorry, Leah. I didn't mean to make such a big mistake.'

Leah hugged Shine. 'It's okay. No mistake is too big to fix. Even one as big as a lake!'

Leah started to inch off the rock. 'Let's get back to dry land so we can practise spinning!' Suddenly, she slipped!

As Leah fell, she bounced off a lily pad and did a perfect ballerina spin!

'I don't know if you meant to do that, but it was amazing!' said Shine.

Leah kept bouncing and spinning from pad to pad. The swans did the same.

'If I keep practising,' she said, 'maybe I'll finally spin like the Swan Queen!'

For the rest of the afternoon, Leah, the genies and the swans practised ballet on the lily pads.

Later in the day, Zac poked his head through
a loose board in the fence. Shimmer and Shine
quickly hid, but he didn't even notice them.

'Whoa!' he shouted to Leah. 'There's a lake
in your backyard!'

Zac had been practising his leaps and was
ready for the show. 'You've got everything we need
– the swans, the Swan Lake and the Swan Queen!'

'I'm still missing one more piece.' Leah held out her hand. 'The best leaper ever! Wanna dance?' Together the two friends put on a magical performance!

After the show, Leah found Shimmer and Shine.
'We fixed our mistakes and the day turned out great!'
She hugged the two genies. 'See you tomorrow?'

'Abso-*genie*-lutely!' chimed Shimmer and Shine.

Treasure Cove Stories

*Book list may be subject to change.